First published in the United States, Great Britain, Canada, Australia, and New Zealand in 2014
by NorthSouth Books Inc., an imprint of NordSüd Verlag AG, CH-8005 Zürich, Switzerland.

Distributed in the United States by NorthSouth Books Inc., New York 10016.
Library of Congress Cataloging-in-Publication Data is available.
Printed in Germany by Grafisches Centrum Cuno GmbH & Co. KG, Calbe, April 2014.
ISBN: 978-0-7358-4178-9
1 3 5 7 9 • 10 8 6 4 2
www.northsouth.com

FSC
www.fsc.org
MIX
Paper from
responsible sources
FSC® C043106

Susanne Löhlein · Henning Löhlein

HAMSTER MONSTER

MINI

PAUL

MAX

NorthSouth

Deep in the forest lived three little hamsters—Max, who was the strongest, Paul, who was the smartest, and Mini, the youngest and littlest.

"Oh, aren't they cute! Oh, aren't they sweet!" people said whenever they saw the three hamsters.

"I've had enough!" shouted Max. "I don't want to be cute and sweet. I want to be mean and scary."

"Yes," said Paul, "let's be mean and scary. Count me in!"

"Me too!" cried Mini. "Me too, me too!"

"Let's frighten people," said Max.

He threw himself into the mud and rolled around. "Look how dirty I am! I look terrifying."

"Wow!" cried Mini. "You look scary!"

Max, Paul, and Mini romped about, throwing mud at each other. They were having fun!

"Being muddy isn't enough." Paul had an idea. "Come on, let's practice glaring."

"What's the point of staring?" asked Mini, always getting confused. But he watched the others and was soon glaring and making scary monster faces, too.

Max, Paul, and Mini hid behind a tree and waited for someone to walk by.

"Attack!" yelled Max.

He and Paul charged out, with Mini chasing after them shouting, "Wait for me! Wait for me!"

Three filthy hamsters leapt onto the path, roaring loudly and making terrifying faces. But the man just kept on walking. He didn't see or hear anything.

"What a disaster! Our faces weren't scary enough.
We need to practice more," said Max.
    "They sure scared me," replied Mini.
    "No, we need to think of something else," said
Paul thoughtfully. "I know! We'll disguise ourselves."

No sooner said than done. They scurried around,
collecting everything they could find on the forest floor.

Dressed up in their wild disguises, Max, Paul, and Mini waited behind the tree once more.

A woman wearing a scarf strolled past.

"Attack!" yelled Max.

"Grrrrr, grrrrr!" roared Paul.

"Oh, nooo!" squealed Mini as he tripped over his costume.

The woman hesitated for a moment, stopped, and then laughed and laughed. Before going on her way, she said, "I've never seen hamsters in such funny costumes. So cute!"

"We're not funny, and we're not cute," grumbled Max to his friends. "We're terrifying hamster monsters."

"Yes, but we haven't actually terrified anyone yet," said Paul.

"Well, I was pretty scared, especially when I fell over," confessed Mini timidly.

Paul thought for a moment. "It's our costumes. They need to be better."

Max, Paul, and Mini set off to make new disguises.

As three boys came walking along the path, Max shouted, "Let's go, gang!"

Paul was right behind Max. Mini bumped into a tree.

The three boys stopped, looked at one another, and then started roaring. *"Raaah!"*

The hamsters panicked. Max jumped right out of his costume, Paul did a back flip, and Mini leapt straight into Max's arms.

"We're just not having any luck," said Max. "Those guys have nerve! We always seem to bump into the wrong sort of people."

"Yeah, I bumped into the wrong sort of people and the tree," said Mini rubbing a big welt on his head.

"We're too little. That's why we're not scaring anyone," explained Paul. "We need to be bigger. Let's build stilts and bigger, scarier costumes. This time we'll do it!"

The hamsters got to work. Soon they were cutting, hammering, and drilling.

Finally, their disguises were ready. Max, Paul, and Mini hid behind the tree and waited.

A little girl was wandering along the forest path.

"Attack!" commanded Max. "And yell as loud as you can!"

They staggered onto the path on their stilts and made a terrible noise.

The little girl was terrified. She took three steps backward and plopped down on the ground.

"We did it!" cheered Max happily. "We're the greatest!"

"Yes, we are mean and scary at last!" said Paul proudly.

But their happiness didn't last long.

"Listen, somebody is crying," said Mini sadly.

The little girl was sobbing. The hamsters took off their costumes and crept toward the girl.

She stopped crying and stood up. With a sly grin, the little girl reached for her zipper . . .

. . . and with a *ZIP!*—revealed that she was a wild, scary monster.

Max, Paul, and Mini were terrified, and they ran away as fast as their little legs could carry them.

"What do you think of my amazing costume?" shouted the monster, giggling to herself.

The three hamsters were safely back in their tree den.

"Why don't we go back to being little, cute, and sweet?" asked Mini.

"Being little is okay," admitted Max. "But why don't we stay just a bit scary?"

"Hmm . . . I've got an idea," said Paul.